A Note to Parents

Read to your child...

★ Reading aloud is one of the best ways to develop your child's love of reading. Read together at least 20 minutes each day.

★ Laughter is contagious! Read with feeling. Show your child that reading is fun.

★ Take time to answer questions your child may have about the story. Linger over pages that interest your child.

...and your child will read to you.

★ Follow cues from your child to know when he wants to join in the reading.

★ Support your young reader. Give him a word whenever he asks for it.

★ Praise your child as he progresses. Your encouraging words will build his confidence.

You can help your Level 1 reader.

★ Reading begins with knowing how a book works. Show your child the title and where the story begins.

★ Ask your child to find picture clues on each page. Talk about what is happening in the story.

★ Point to the words as you read so your child can make the connection between the print and the story.

★ Ask your child to point to words she knows.

★ Let your child supply the rhyming words.

Most of all, enjoy your reading time together!

**—Bernice Cullinan, Ph.D.,
Professor of Reading, New York University**

Reader's Digest Children's Books
Reader's Digest Road, Pleasantville, NY 10570-7000 and
Reader's Digest Children's Publishing Limited,
The Ice House, 124-126 Walcot Street, Bath UK BA1 5BG
Copyright © 1999 Reader's Digest Children's Publishing, Inc.
All rights reserved. Reader's Digest Children's Books is a trademark
and Reader's Digest and All-Star Readers are registered trademarks
of the Reader's Digest Association, Inc.
Printed in China.
ISBN: 0-7944-0237-2
Library of Congress Number: 98-49565
10 9 8 7 6 5 4 3 2 1

When I Am Big

by Mary Packard
illustrated by Laura Rader

1

All-Star Readers®

Reader's Digest Children's Books™

Pleasantville, New York • Montréal, Québec

When I am big,
I will ride a big bike.

I will play lots of sports,

like my big brother, Mike.

When I am big,
I will run lots of races.

I will score lots of goals

and steal lots of bases.

When I am big,

I will be very strong.

I will skate on one leg

and play hard all day long.

When I am big,

I will be very quick.

I will run. I will pass.

I will block.

I will kick.

When I am big,

I will be VERY tall.

But for now I have Mike,

so I'm tall after all.

Color in the star next to each word you can read.

☆ a	☆ have	☆ quick
☆ after	☆ I	☆ races
☆ all	☆ I'm	☆ ride
☆ am	☆ kick	☆ run
☆ and	☆ leg	☆ score
☆ bases	☆ like	☆ skate
☆ be	☆ long	☆ so
☆ big	☆ lots	☆ sports
☆ bike	☆ Mike	☆ steal
☆ block	☆ my	☆ strong
☆ brother	☆ now	☆ tall
☆ but	☆ of	☆ when
☆ day	☆ on	☆ will
☆ for	☆ one	☆ very
☆ goals	☆ pass	
☆ hard	☆ play	